Sunshine

A Level One Reader

By Alice K. Flanagan

NEW HANOVER COUNTY
PUBLIC LIBRARY
201 CHESTNUT STREET
WILMINGTON, NC 28401

The
Child's
World®

How do you feel on a warm sunny day?

Sunshine warms our skin and makes us feel good.

Sunshine helps animals and plants grow.

What is the sun made of?

The sun is a hot ball of burning gas.

Without light from the sun, our world would be dark.

Without heat from the sun, our world would be cold.

We need the sun.

Be sure to protect yourself from the sun's strong rays.

Don't stay out in the sun too long!

Word List

burning

gas

protect

rays

skin

sunshine

world

Note to Parents and Educators

Welcome to Wonder Books®! These books provide text at three different levels for beginning readers to practice and strengthen their reading skills. Additionally, the use of nonfiction text provides readers the valuable opportunity to *read to learn*, not just to learn to read.

These leveled readers allow children to choose books at their level of reading confidence and performance. Nonfiction Level One books offer beginning readers simple language, word choice, and sentence structure as well as a word list. Nonfiction Level Two books feature slightly more difficult vocabulary, longer sentences, and longer total text. In the back of each Nonfiction Level Two book are an index and a list of books and Web sites for finding out more information. Nonfiction Level Three books continue to extend word choice and length of text. In the back of each Nonfiction Level Three book are a glossary, an index, and a list of books and Web sites for further research.

State and national standards in reading and language arts emphasize using nonfiction at all levels of reading development. Wonder Books® fill the historical void in nonfiction material for the primary grade readers with the additional benefit of a leveled text.

About the Author

Alice K. Flanagan taught elementary school for ten years. Now she writes for children and teachers. She has been writing for more than twenty years. Some of her books include biographies, phonics books, holiday books, and information books about careers, animals, and weather. Alice K. Flanagan lives with her husband in Chicago, Illinois.

Published by The Child's World®
P.O. Box 326
Chanhassen, MN 55317-0326
800-599-READ
www.childsworld.com

Photo Credits
© Allan Shoemaker/Taxi: 21
© Ariel Skelley/CORBIS: 6
© CORBIS: 13
© David Madison/Tony Stone: 17
© Gary Cralle/The Image Bank: 14
© Pat Powers & Cherryl Schafer/PhotoDisc: cover
© Peter Cade/Tony Stone: 18
© Roger Ressmeyer/CORBIS: 10
© Rolf Bruderer/CORBIS: 2
© Silvestre Machado/Tony Stone: 9
© SW Productions/PhotoDisc: 5

Editorial Directions, Inc.: E. Russell Primm and Emily J. Dolbear, Editors;
Alice K. Flanagan, Photo Research; Emily J. Dolbear, Photo Selector

The Child's World®: Mary Berendes, Publishing Director

Copyright © 2003 by The Child's World®
All rights reserved. No part of this book may be
reproduced or utilized in any form or by any means
without written permission from the publisher.
Printed in the United States of America.

Library of Congress Cataloging-in-Publication Data
Flanagan, Alice K.
  Sunshine / by Alice K. Flanagan.
    p. cm. — (Wonder books)
Summary: Simple text describes the sun, its characteristics, and its
beneficial impacts on the Earth.
Includes bibliographical references and index.
  ISBN 1-56766-454-7 (lib. bdg. : alk. paper)
  1. Sun—Juvenile literature. 2. Sunshine—Juvenile literature. [1.
Sun.] I. Title. II. Series: Wonder books (Chanhassen, Minn.)
  QB521.5 .F56 2003
  523.7—dc21
                        2002151613

24

ML